Woody's Wonderful World

by

Cécile Curtis

McGraw-Hill Book Company
New York · San Francisco

First distribution in the United States
of America by McGraw-Hill Book Company, 1967
Library of Congress Catalog Card Number: AC 67-10512

First published by Hodder and Stoughton Ltd., 1964
Copyright © by Cécile Curtis, 1964

Printed in Great Britain

To My Father

RICHARD S. NEWBOLD

Who always encouraged me
to draw animals.

With my gratitude and affection.

U. S. 1406485

This is the story of Woody a field mouse who lived in the bushes and tall grasses of Primrose Hill in London.

There really wouldn't have been much to tell about him if it hadn't been for that little white patch of fur on top of his head. You see, Woody was different from all the other mice around about. Not one of his brothers or sisters, aunts, uncles or cousins, had a white patch on their heads.

Now, you wouldn't think that this would really matter,

9

but as Woody grew up he noticed more and more that all the other little field mice seemed to leave him on his own, and he had nobody to play with.

They would gather together in little groups, whispering and laughing at him.

"What a funny looking fellow he is," they would say.

"Who ever heard of a mouse with a white patch like his?"—and so on until Woody became more and more lonely and often had to brush a tear from his big shiny black eyes.

One day, on a morning when the sun was shining brightly in the treetops and the sweet smell of dew was on the ground, Woody decided that he would leave the field that had been his home and go out and see the world.

He waited, trembling, by the side of the great wide road where the cars rushed up and down and when the ugly noisy things had passed and everything was quiet for a moment he scurried as quickly as his little legs would carry him over to the other side.

He was away!

It was easy enough for him to find a little opening in the high railings in front of him and in he dashed.

He found himself in a lovely sort of garden, not a bit like the place he had just left. Around him were wonderful buildings and all kinds of exciting noises that he had never heard before.

Strange birdcalls filled the air with music and blended with animal voices all around. Through the trees came the sound of happy jungle laughter and contented growling seemed to be saying that here was peace and plenty.

There were streams and ponds and tall trees. Big boats passed by on the canal, filled with people who were all having such a good time.

There were so many interesting smells too. For a moment Woody did not quite know which way to go. He could see a path near by and people walking along but they were so busy looking at all the cages that nobody noticed a little mouse in the bushes – not even a little mouse with a white patch on his head.

Little Woody, in his headlong dash into the big wide world, had landed himself right in the middle of the Zoo.

What a wonderful place it was!

All kinds of flowers grew around the great soaring cages in which Woody could see bright feathered birds flying gaily about or looking at the people who passed in front of them. Woody saw that the cages had bars or netting to keep the people out. What a lovely idea!

He wandered on over the bridge easily dodging the feet of the passers-by.

"Perhaps here I can find some friends who won't make fun of me," thought Woody.

Along the edge of the bright flower beds he ran, hoping to find someone who would talk with him.

Out of the corner of his eye he noticed four thin tree trunks right in the middle of a large open space. They were white with orange patches and not like any he had ever seen before. He hurried over to the base of one and stared up at its great height, his eyes blinking in the bright sun. He wondered what sort of leaves such strange trees would have and decided to climb one.

As he scurried up the soft smooth bark he thought that the wind was much stronger here as the tree trunks now seemed to be swaying gently.

There was also a crunching noise in the leaves. He pushed one aside to see what had caused this and nearly fell over backward with surprise.

There he was, face to face with Grumpy the giraffe!

"Oh my goodness!" said Woody, feeling very foolish.

Grumpy, who was just about to gobble up the leaves around the little mouse, suddenly caught sight of the white furry patch on his head and stopped just in time.

"Hullo," she said, "So that's what I felt tickling my leg! Who are you and what are you doing here, little one?"

Woody was very shy in front of such a grand creature but felt better when he saw the kind look in her large black eyes and found himself telling her all about his home and why he had run away to find friends.

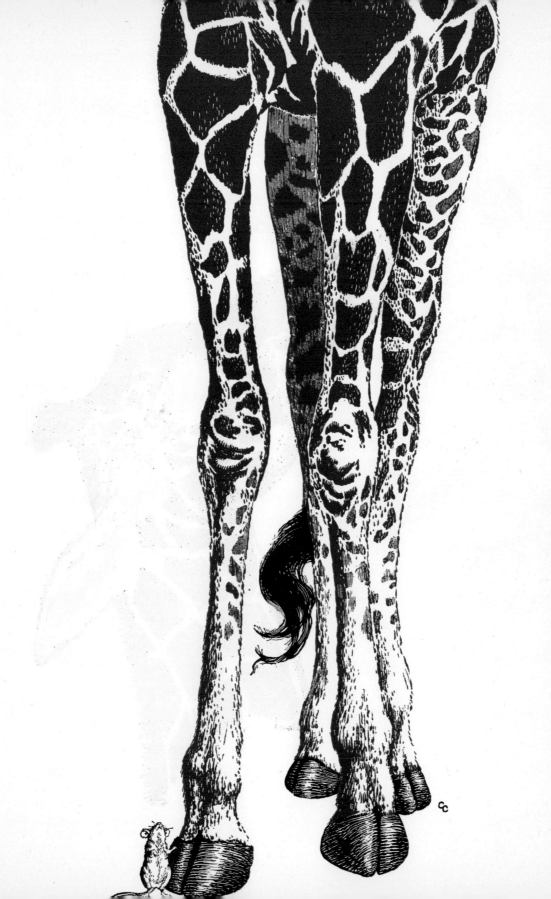

Grumpy listened sympathetically, chewing her leaves all the while, until Woody began to wonder if there would be anything left on which he could balance. He was also feeling a bit dizzy as he was not used to looking down from such a height.

"I really should be getting along now," said Woody, "thank you very much for talking with me, Mrs. Giraffe."

Grumpy made a soft murmuring noise in her throat and Woody politely made his way down to the ground, this time using the post that supported the basket and the leaves.

Whiskered nose scenting the air, Woody strolled slowly back toward the bridge where a boat was stopping.

Just ahead was the most enormous creature Woody had ever seen, and behind it were two more!

Elephants!

Oh, how big they were!

They were being fed by a group of children, and Woody could only just see the tops of their heads as they reached down to take the food, but they had no white patch. They were just a nice gray color and seemed so gentle in spite of their size. One of them saw Woody, for elephants have very sharp eyes, and waved her trunk in such a friendly way. Woody watched the children giving them buns and apples and realized what a lovely place this was, where one did not have to go and search for food but where people actually gave you all sorts of delicious things to eat.

He would have liked to have
talked to the elephants but he
couldn't see how he could get any-
where near them. Remembering
how uncomfortable he had been

16

up there with the giraffe, he thought it best not to try.

He turned back in the direction of a large tunnel and raced through its long dark length.

The sun was so bright when he came out at the other end of it that he ducked into the first building that he saw. It was even darker here than the tunnel had been and when he looked around Woody got another surprise!

All about were lighted tanks of water with hundreds of different kinds of fish racing up and down in them.

Woody ran along a narrow ledge peering in at this strange watery world. A particularly big fish swam right up so close to him that he tumbled off the ledge, he was so amazed. This was surely not a place where he could find someone to talk with.

He looked for the light of the doorway and darted quickly outside. Over there was a building which looked more promising. He would try that.

He scampered across the path and in through the open door.

Small, brightly lit cages lined the walls and everywhere was the gay chatter and friendliness which he wanted so much. Bright round eyes peered out at him and long tails waved a welcome.

"Good morning."

"Hullo there."

"Come on in and join us."

"Have a peanut."

Woody felt at home immediately. All these happy folk were pleased to see him. Invitations were called from all sides and nobody seemed to notice his funny white patch. He didn't know which way to turn.

The first animal he noticed was sitting all by herself on a thick branch.

She was a bright reddish color with the longest tail he had ever seen. It was not thin and pink like his but wonderfully fluffy with bright yellow stripes.

"I'm Katey the tree kangaroo and I'm very unusual," she

said proudly when she saw the little mouse admiring her. "I come all the way from New Guinea."

"New Guinea?" said Woody, looking puzzled; "is that near Primrose Hill?"

All the animals laughed, but in the nicest possible way so that Woody really didn't mind a bit.

"It's all the way over on the other side of the world, and so is India where I come from."

Woody looked up to see who was speaking now.

Next to Katey was a very strange creature indeed. He looked just like a fox with wings but the oddest thing of all was that he was hanging upside down from the top of his cage!

Woody climbed up to the wire mesh above him and looked down at Gunga Din the Indian fruit bat. He still couldn't see him very well, so he tried hanging upside down by his feet too. The fruit bat certainly did look more natural from this angle and besides, it seemed to Woody to be the polite way to talk to him.

"Do tell us about Primrose Hill," said Gunga Din.

He was just about to answer when he felt his paws slipping and pulled himself right side up just in time.

"Well sir," said Woody, when he was safely on the ground again, "I ran away from my home on Primrose Hill because none of the other little mice would play with me. You see, they haven't got a white patch on their heads and they all make fun of me."

19

"Well they must be very silly mice," said the bush baby, looking down at Woody with big thoughtful eyes.

"What a shame," added the mongoose. "Such a nice little fellow should have lots of playmates."

The armadillo up at the other end of the room shook his armor-like covering and studied Woody.

"What a lovely coat he has," he said in a squeaky voice, "so silky and soft, and with that pretty little white patch on his head. Really a most handsome mouse, I do declare."

The flying squirrel swung across to his nest and after rummaging about came back with a grape. He put a tiny hand out to Woody.

"Here you are. Please take this."

"Thank you very much sir," said Woody.

He nibbled away while around him the animals called to one another.

For the first time in his life Woody felt no need to be ashamed of his odd coloring. He sat back holding the grape between his front paws and felt a warm glow in the company of his new-found friends. They approved his long whiskers and his black shining eyes, they remarked respectfully upon his delicate pink nose and his fine rose-petal ears. But most of all they admired the white patch of fur upon his head.

Two little figures with long pointed noses and striped fur clung to the fine mesh of their cage, chattering to him eagerly. These were ring-tailed coati-mundis from South America.

"Come over to our house little fellow," said one of them, who was called Don Pancho. "Look, we have nuts and fruit and all sorts of things to eat."

Woody scampered over to join them and had a lovely time playing follow-the-leader with these frisky friends. He soon found that he could not keep up with them, however, and jumped into the next cage which seemed to be empty except for what he thought was a large thorny bush in one corner.

The bush shook itself and stretched out and suddenly there was Porky, the giant crested porcupine grinning at him and showing two big yellow teeth.

"Have some breakfast with me," said Porky. "As you can see, there's more than enough here."

The mouse could just reach over the top of the big plate of lettuce and fruit. They were truly delicious.

After they had eaten, Porky showed Woody how he could roll up into a ball and rattle his quills most effectively, and the two of them spent a pleasant time chatting of this and that.

By now Woody had just about decided that this was the nicest place he had seen and that he could settle down here with all these happy creatures forever. His thoughts were suddenly interrupted.

There was a loud bang as a door was pushed open and all at once the room was filled with children. They shouted to one another as they tried to find places in front of Porky's cage, pushing each other aside to get a better view.

The sound of their voices was deafening in this closed in space and although the building had seemed to be full, more kept coming in and the big doors banged again and again adding to the din.

With a quick leap Woody bounded out of the porcupine's cage, somehow managing to dodge the hundreds of feet, and in the twinkling of an eye he was once more outside in the warm sunshine.

"Ah, this is better," he thought as he hopped along, not taking much notice of where he was going, but grateful to find space in which to run without the noise and bustle he had just escaped. It had been so nice finding all those friendly animals but he did wish there had been some place where he could have hidden from that noisy crowd.

He suddenly forgot all about them when he caught sight of what was probably the oddest animal he had yet seen.

24

Its long fur hung down almost to the ground in broad bands of black, white and gray. The puzzling thing was that at both ends its body was long and pointed and to Woody looked exactly the same, and since the creature remained still he couldn't tell if it were coming or going!

This unusual fellow was in fact Anthony, the giant ant-eater from South America, but Woody never found this out. He would have liked to have had a word with him but since he couldn't make out which end he should speak to, he thought better of it and went on his way.

He remembered seeing a cage with some black bears when he had first come outside again. Yes, there they were! But now they were all curled up fast asleep so he passed them by as well.

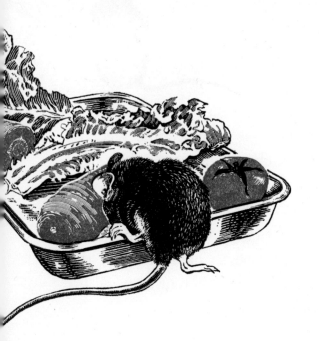

Further along was a large walled-in place with a thick black tire hanging from a tree in the center.

One quick leap onto the wall and down the other side and he was looking up at Chi-chi, the giant panda from China.

When she saw the little mouse she dropped the piece of
bamboo that she had been busily chewing.

"What have we here?" said she, bending down to have a
better look at him.

"My name is Woody and I've run away from home to
find some friends." And he went on to explain about the
white patch on his head that made him different from all his
brothers and sisters, aunts, uncles and cousins.

"Well, I think your white patch makes you look very hand-

some, rather like me really," Chi-chi said. "If it weren't for my unusual patches I wouldn't be nearly so famous. Just look at all those people staring at me."

Sure enough the wall around them was lined with crowds of people all trying to get a better look.

Woody felt very proud to be compared with such a fine creature and would have been happy to go on talking with her all day. But Chi-chi suddenly straightened up as a keeper entered her enclosure.

"Here comes my keeper to play with me," she said; "he comes to have a romp with me every day, so I don't ever feel lonely for very long." And she bounded off to greet him.

Woody called out good-bye to her and rather sadly went on his way once more.

He darted across wide lawns past a great crowd of people who were watching the chimp's tea party, past bright cockatoos and graceful gibbons swinging like acrobats in their high cages. He hopped along a branch trying to copy them but to his disgust a Hoopoe bird mistook him for one of her young and tried to feed him a big fat worm. Luckily for him she soon realized her mistake and flew away.

Woody tripped gaily on thrilled by all he saw. Then, without warning and not realizing why, he was suddenly afraid. He stopped. All was silent. He looked up.

There, in a vast cage towering above him, beady eyes stared down. Over there were more. They were all around him. Woody was so frightened! Half-forgotten warnings by his parents came back to him. Warnings of just such piercing eyes, sharp beaks and clasping talons.

29

Giant birds! Eagles!

Poor Woody. He ran and ran and ran. Down the path past the rows of watching eyes, frantically avoiding the clumsy crowds who seemed to bar his way.

He was in such a hurry that he very nearly ran right into the long pink leg of a majestic flamingo who in turn let out a loud undignified squawk of alarm.

"Oh dear me, Mr. Flamingo, I do beg your pardon sir," gasped Woody, by now feeling a bit silly when he looked up and saw that the eagles weren't really after him at all.

30

The tall flamingo shook himself delicately. "That's all right little mouse, but mind how you go around here if you don't want to get into trouble." And with that he balanced himself with ease on one leg and tucked his head under his wing.

Woody promised to be very careful and said good-bye, although he didn't think the flamingo could have heard.

He followed along the edge of a pond with three little islands in its center taking care not to run into any more flamingoes. There were certainly enough of them here. They looked like big pink flowers clustered along the water's edge.

Woody continued his wandering along a long line of paddocks. He passed some buffalo who were sitting in the shade of their house, and near them a funny looking chap called a yak who turned up his nose in the most haughty fashion when Woody tried to make conversation.

Then he came to the last house of all. Looking through the railings at the rather muddy enclosure he could see no sign of movement.

Of course, being so small Woody could not see very far. Right in the middle of the paddock was a large rock behind which someone might be sleeping. He would climb up the

rock and take a look from there. He approached cautiously and tested the air. There were so many strange smells about that he wasn't quite sure which was which, but one smell seemed to be nearer than the others.

Woody started to climb up the side. It was steep to begin with but then flattened out. He came to a sharp point in the rock. From the top of that he would be able to see all round. Taking a firm grip with his paws he began to climb.

Suddenly the rock started to move, gently at first and then more violently. It rose from the surrounding mud and Woody clung desperately to his hold. All at once two large eyes with thick black lashes appeared from nowhere just in front of him, blinked once or twice and then stared at him in surprise. Somewhere below him a voice spoke, rumbling from the depths of a mighty throat, and Woody saw that the thing he was clinging to was part of some huge animal.

It had not been a rock at all he had climbed but the animal himself, and now he was actually on the horn that stuck out of the creature's nose! It was Ben, the rhinoceros.

"And who are you, may I ask?" said the voice, nearly shaking Woody from his uneasy perch.

"I— I'm Woody if you please sir, Woody the field mouse."

"You are, are you," replied the rhinoceros, "and what is it you want, disturbing my afternoon nap?"

Woody held on more tightly than ever. Obviously Mr. Ben was a little bit angry.

33

"If you please Mr. Ben, I'm just looking for some friendly folk. I never had any friends at home on Primrose Hill because all the other mice laughed at the strange white patch on top of my head."

The rhinoceros lifted his horn very slightly so that Woody was carried higher still. He studied Woody carefully. First he closed one eye and then the other, and finally looked up at him with both, turning his huge head from side to side.

"Hmmmm. In my opinion it looks very nice, not strange at all, in fact I couldn't imagine you without it."

At these comforting words from this mighty creature Woody felt very pleased.

Ben was really very kind in spite of his rather frightening appearance. Woody only wished his home were more comfortable. He was feeling rather tired after all his travels and there was no warm dry spot where a little mouse could curl up for a nap. Nothing here in fact except mud and more mud.

Woody thought how nice it would be if he could make his home with one of the many animals here. Someone who would be glad of company and whose house could provide him with just a small corner that was warm and dark and dry where he could hide himself sometimes when there was too much noise.

Woody heaved a tiny sigh at this thought. He just didn't have any idea where he might find such a place.

The rhinoceros looked as if he might be going back to sleep again.

"Thank you very much sir for talking with me," said Woody. "May I please get down now?"

"Why, of course," said Mr. Ben, "I'll just lie down again and then you can climb off easily."

So Mr. Ben gently lay down and put his head on the ground and Woody jumped off.

For the first time he was really able to see the rhinoceros' great bulk. He was nearly as big as the elephant, or so it seemed to the tiny mouse.

Still lying down Mr. Ben turned his eyes in Woody's direction.

"Good-bye Woody," he said, closing his eyes once more.

Woody tiptoed softly away out of the enclosure. On the other side of the railings he sat down and carefully brushed all the mud off his legs.

Some distance away he could see another big animal that he had missed earlier and he went over for a closer look.

Although Woody had seen a number of animals by now, including some very unusual ones indeed, he was still taken by surprise to see one with two humps on its back. He watched it from a distance for some time then came forward and introduced himself.

"How do you do Woody," replied the camel. "My name is Alice, and I am pleased to meet you."

While talking, Alice chewed slowly and noisily and made rather peculiar sounds in her throat.

"All I can offer you," she continued, "is some hay. It's really very good hay. Try some."

Woody shook his head.

"No thank you Miss Alice, as a matter of fact I had a late breakfast and am not really hungry."

"I'm not hungry myself," explained the camel, "but I always eat when I have the chance and then store the food in these humps of mine that you see on my back."

She paused and took another mouthful of hay.

"Of course, living here and eating regularly I do not really need to store food but in my home in the desert there are long periods when there is just nothing to eat at all."

"How interesting!" exclaimed Woody. "But why do you have two humps when your friend over there has only one?"

Alice laughed, with a deep funny rumbling.

"He's related to me but comes from a different part of the world altogether. His home is really in Africa where it is hot, that's why he has such a short coat, whereas my family live in a cold climate and have this nice long woolly fur."

"I see," said Woody.

At that moment one of the keepers came toward them with several children following him.

"It's time for me to take the children for rides on my back so I'll have to leave you now."

The camel moved off in a slow dignified way chewing her hay all the while.

Our little friend waved good-bye with a tiny pink paw and took off in the general direction of the seal pond.

He was feeling very thirsty with all this running about, so arriving at the pond the first thing he did was to put his head down to the surface of the water. He almost fell right in with astonishment when a smooth shiny head poked up in front of his nose with a gurgled "Good morning." It disappeared just as suddenly only to pop up again at the opposite side.

That seemed very clever! He wished he could join in the fun.

It was then that he saw the little round boat. It was floating right at the edge of the water and as he went over to inspect it he saw that it had a small wooden paddle, just the right size for a mouse!

He climbed in and the boat bobbed merrily on the surface of the pond which looked more like a big lake to Woody. At first the boat just went round in circles but after a little practice he was able to make it move where he wanted.

Millie the seal swam toward him.

"And where do you think you're going?" she asked.

"Well, I don't really know," was the answer. "I guess I'm trying to get to the other side."

His short arms were beginning to get very tired although he had hardly traveled any distance at all.

"I'll blow bubbles behind your boat and you'll glide across the water easily," Millie said.

With her blowing and Woody paddling as fast as his little arms would go they soon arrived on the other bank, and there he hopped out, glad to be on firm ground once more.

He thanked the kind seal for helping him, wondering all the while what it must be like to live in the water all the time.

Suddenly the pond seemed to be filled with seals as they all

rose to the surface at once to watch a keeper putting fish into a metal box by the side of the water. As soon as he had finished, there came the sound of a motor and the fun started. The box moved around on a track at great speed scattering the fish, and the seals chased after it eagerly, catching them so quickly that Woody could hardly see them at all.

He moved away cautiously to avoid getting wet but he might just as well not have bothered.

Before he knew where he was he found himself in the middle of a puddle surrounded by big black and white birds whose smooth feathers glistened with water. They were King penguins and they towered over the little mouse.

One of them must have mistaken him for a baby penguin for she bent her head down to this little furry creature tucked between her large wrinkled feet as though she were trying to protect him from the others.

Woody let out a shrill squeak as a cold drop of water fell from her beak right on to the white furry patch on his head.

This was altogether too much for him and he made a hasty escape.

On and on he ran, past the raccoons and the lion house, passed the rows of antelopes and the giant anteater.

Only then did he slow down and start to notice things around him once more.

There was a good deal of loud chattering coming from a line

of cages just ahead and he looked up with interest at all the different monkeys.

Then it was that he saw Guy the gorilla. He was so enormous that he didn't look as though he belonged with all these little monkeys. He was sitting quietly on a big bed of straw skillfully shelling a peanut.

Woody tiptoed into the corner of his cage marveling at the great barrel-like chest and the long powerful arms.

Suddenly he saw Guy looking at him.

"What kind eyes he has!" thought Woody and drew closer.

The gorilla watched him without moving, then gently put out one great black finger and stroked the white furry patch on his head. He opened his huge hand and the mouse climbed trustingly on to it.

"What a lovely little mouse!" he said, slowly lifting him up.

"I notice Mr. Gorilla, sir, that all the others here have lots of companions to play with, but since you are all on your own I took the liberty of coming in to join you."

"I'm so glad you did, as I do get bored sometimes and it's fine to be able to talk to someone. You know, I would not have noticed you at all had it not been for that little white patch of fur on your head."

Woody told him how he was different from his brothers and sisters, aunts and uncles and cousins, and why he had run away from home.

"Well, I've never actually seen a field mouse before, so that

as far as I'm concerned you are just what a field mouse should look like."

On hearing this Woody felt so happy and snuggled trustingly into the gorilla's great palm.

"Would you like something to eat, little mouse?" asked Guy.

"Thank you very much, Mr. Gorilla, just a very tiny piece of something will be enough for me."

Guy gave him the tiniest piece of banana his big fingers could break off and popped the rest of it into his mouth.

Woody told him about all his adventures and of how he had been seeking friends and a nice home.

"Why here's the place, surely," said Guy. "I have this big house out here and another one inside as well with plenty of nice soft straw everywhere. There's even a thick glass wall between me and all the crowds of people so you won't be frightened by the noise."

Woody thought this sounded just perfect and snuggled down contentedly into the palm of the gorilla's hand. He closed his eyes at last for the nap that he needed so much, happy with the thought that finally he had found a real home.

Now whenever you go to the Zoo, remember to look around you very carefully, for you just might be lucky enough to see a most unusual sight— a little mouse with a white furry patch on top of his head.

1088